PRIVATE AND CONFIDENTIAL

Marion Ripley

Illustrated by

Colin Backhouse

FRANCES LINCOLN

"What does PRIVATE AND CONFIDENTIAL mean?" asked Laura. "There's a letter here for Mum and it's written on the envelope in big black letters."

Joe was opening his newsletter from the local football club.

"It means that no one else is allowed to read it except Mum," he said. "It's probably from the bank."

"It's not fair," said Laura. "Why doesn't anyone ever write to me?"

The next day at school, Mr Joshi made an announcement.
"I've had a letter from a teacher in Australia," he said.
"If any of you would like an Australian penfriend,
come and see me."

Laura was really excited. She hurried up to Mr Joshi's classroom.

"Can I have a girl who likes swimming, gerbils and watching television?" she said.

"I'm sorry, Laura," said Mr Joshi, "all the children are boys. You can have Steve, Paul, Darren, Malcolm or Luke."

Laura was a bit disappointed. "Never mind," she said, "I'll have Malcolm."

That night Laura sat down to write her first letter to Malcolm. It was hard to know what to say.

“Just tell him about yourself and ask him to write back. That’s enough to start with,” said Dad.

So that’s what she did.

Dear Malcolm,

I got your address from a teacher at my school. I am ten years old and go to Hollyridge School. I like Swimming and watching television and talking to my friends. Sometimes I get into trouble because I talk in class and in assembly and other times I'm not supposed to!

I would really like a letter from you. please Send me a photo if you can.

What is it like living in Australia?

from
Laura O'Brien

Laura waited for the post every day and it was not long before an airmail letter arrived for her – all the way from Australia!

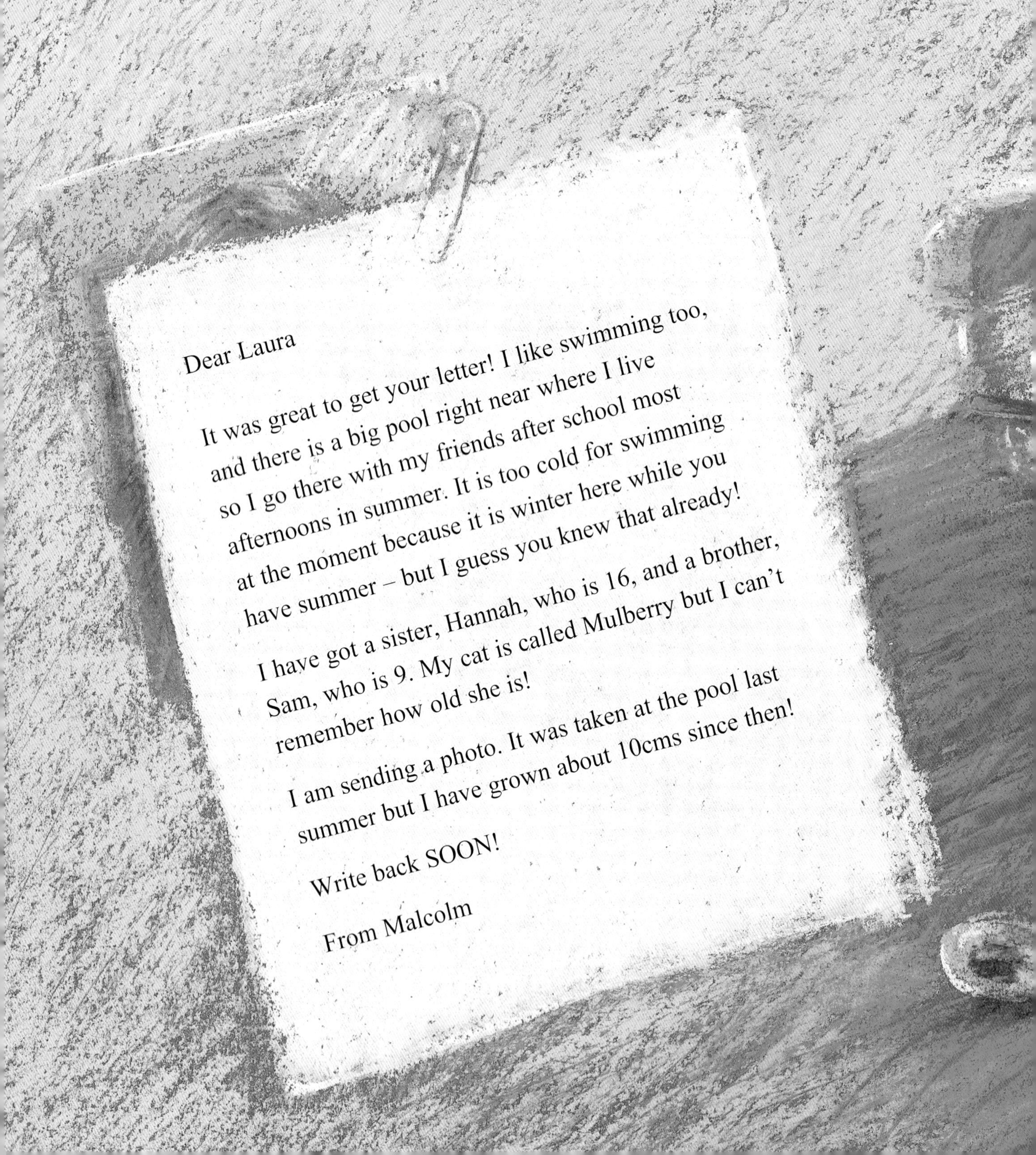

Dear Laura

It was great to get your letter! I like swimming too, and there is a big pool right near where I live so I go there with my friends after school most afternoons in summer. It is too cold for swimming at the moment because it is winter here while you have summer – but I guess you knew that already!

I have got a sister, Hannah, who is 16, and a brother, Sam, who is 9. My cat is called Mulberry but I can't remember how old she is!

I am sending a photo. It was taken at the pool last summer but I have grown about 10cms since then!

Write back SOON!

From Malcolm

Laura really liked the letter and she really liked the photo. She took them into school and got told off for passing them round in Assembly.

That evening she wrote a long letter to Malcolm and sent him a photo even though he hadn't actually asked for one. At the end of the letter she wrote "Write back SOON!"

She posted it on her way to school the next morning.

Laura waited and waited
for a reply from Malcolm,
and after three weeks she still
hadn't heard from him.
It was really disappointing.

"Perhaps he didn't like your
photo," said Joe.

At last there was a letter! But it wasn't from Malcolm.

Dear Laura

I'm Malcolm's sister and I'm writing to you because I think you might be waiting for a letter from him.

He has had to go into hospital for an eye operation. He has very poor sight – in fact he can hardly see at all and he never will be able to. He goes to the same school as the rest of us but he types most of his work and his lesson books are in Braille.

I read your letters to him and I described your photo. He thought you sounded really nice and he has shown the photo to all his friends!

He should be out of hospital next week and I'm sure he'll write to you then.

Love from Hannah

"What's up, Laura?" asked Dad as he came into the hall.

"It's Malcolm," said Laura. "He's nearly blind. He's gone into hospital for an operation but it isn't going to make him see any better. I can't believe it. Why didn't he tell me?"

"Perhaps he didn't think it was the most important thing about him," said Dad. "Maybe he wanted to talk about swimming, and his family, and the cat instead. He was probably going to tell you when you knew each other a bit better. Does it really make that much difference?"

Laura got out the photo of Malcolm.
He looked so fit and happy in the picture,
it was hard to imagine him being ill
in hospital. Then she had an idea.
She would send him a Get Well card,
and she would do it in braille!

Karen at school had an auntie who
was blind. She would probably help if
she was not too busy with her baby.

After school the next day, Laura went
with Karen to visit her auntie.
Karen's auntie had a brailling machine
which was a bit like a typewriter but with
fewer keys. She gave Laura a braille
alphabet card and showed her how to press
the keys so that they made raised dots.
Then she put Laura's card in the brailler
and Laura brailled her message:

Get Well Soon
Love from Laura

Ten days later a letter arrived. But it wasn't a pale blue airmail envelope this time. It was a cardboard tube with a special address label on the outside. Inside the tube was a letter – IN BRAILLE! Laura sat down on the stairs with her alphabet card to find out what it said.

a	b	c	d	e	f	g	h	i	j	k	l	m
n	o	p	q	r	s	t	u	v	w	x	y	z

Full stop

Question Mark

Exclamation mark

"What does your letter say?" asked Joe, peering over Laura's shoulder.

"I'm not telling you," said Laura. "From now on, my letters from Malcolm are Private and Confidential!"

For school use:

Here is Malcolm's braille letter. Using the alphabet card below, can you find out what it says?

a b c d e f g h i j k l m

n o p q r s t u v w x y z

Full stop   Question Mark   Exclamation mark

Some facts about braille

Braille was invented by a French man called Louis Braille. He was blind because of an injury from one of his father's sharp tools when he was just three years old. He went on to become a teacher and died in 1852.

There are approximately 1.5 million blind children in the world. Almost 1000 children in the UK read and write in braille. Some of these children cannot see at all. Others have some sight but not enough to read print, even if it is very large.

Braille is based on cells of up to six raised dots. Capital letters can be shown by adding an extra dot before the letter. The capital sign is not used in Malcolm's letter to make it easier to read. Braille readers run their fingers lightly over the dots to read the words.

The braille in this book is grade 1 braille, which is the simplest kind. Most books in braille are in grade 2 braille, which is quicker to read but more difficult to learn. Different braille codes are used in other languages, including Arabic and Japanese. Braille can also be used for music and mathematics.

Some blind people use special computers where the writing on the screen is converted into braille dots on a panel under the reader's fingers. Others use computers with a voice synthesiser which reads aloud everything on the screen. In this way, people who cannot see can send and receive email, and use the Internet.

If you liked this story and would like a penfriend yourself, why not contact *Write Away*? This is an organisation which runs penfriend clubs for both children and adults, including those with special needs. For further details, contact them at their address below.

Some useful addresses:

Write Away
1 Thorpe Close
London
W10 5XL

www.write-away.org

Royal National Institute of the Blind
105 Judd Street
London
WC1H 9NE

www.rnib.org.uk

Vision Australia Foundation
454 Glenferrie Road
Kooyong
VIC 3144
Australia

www.visionaustralia.org.au

Here is the translation of Malcolm's letter. Did you get it right?

Dear Laura

Thank you for the card. Can we be brailler pals instead of pen pals?

Write back soon! Love from Malcolm